MARTY FRYE PRIVATE EYE

THE CASE OF THE MISSING ACTION FIGURE & OTHER MYSTERIES

ACTION CHUCK

BOOK ONE

MARTY PRIVATE EYE

FRYE

THE CASE OF THE MISSING ACTION FIGURE

& OTHER MYSTERIES

JANET TASHJIAN

illustrated by **LAURIE KELLER**

Christy Ottaviano Books
Henry Holt and Company · New York

Henry Holt and Company
Publishers since 1866
175 Fifth Avenue
New York, New York 10010
mackids.com

Henry Holt® is a registered trademark of Macmillan Publishing Group, LLC.
Text copyright © 1998 by Janet Tashjian
Illustrations copyright © 1998 by Laurie Keller
All rights reserved.

Library of Congress Cataloging-in-Publication Data
Tashjian, Janet.
Marty Frye, Private Eye/by Janet Tashjian;
illustrated by Laurie Keller.
p.   cm.
Summary: Marty Frye, a seven-year-old who likes to read poetry and talk in rhymes, solves
three separate mysteries for a classmate, a toy store owner, and his younger sister.
[1. Mystery and detective stories. 2. Poets—Fiction.]
I. Keller, Laurie, ill. II. Title.
PZ7. T211135Mar   1998   [Fic]—dc21   98-13770

ISBN 978-1-250-11661-1

Our books may be purchased in bulk for promotional, educational, or business use. Please
contact your local bookseller or the Macmillan Corporate and Premium Sales Department
at (800) 221-7945 ext. 5442 or by e-mail at MacmillanSpecialMarkets@macmillan.com.

First Edition—1998
Revised Henry Holt Edition—2017

Printed in the United States of America by LSC Communications, Crawfordsville, Indiana

1 3 5 7 9 10 8 6 4 2

For Josh Levison—a true poet

—J. T.

To my grandmother,
Evelyn Luella
—L. K.

CONTENTS

MARTY FRYE PRIVATE EYE

THE CASE OF THE MISSING ACTION FIGURE

& OTHER MYSTERIES

THE CASE OF THE MISSING DIARY

THE CRIME

It was recess, and Marty Frye was hungry. He climbed his favorite tree. He began to peel an orange. His classmate Emma stopped him.

"Come down!" she yelled. "Someone stole my diary, and you have to find it!"

Marty put his orange away. He climbed down the tree. He gave Emma his card. It was written in crayon on the back of a milk carton.

"This is so messy I can hardly read it," Emma said. "Does it say PET detective?"

"No," Marty said.

"Does it say PLANT detective?"

"No," Marty repeated.

"Does it say PILOT detective?"

"NO!" Marty screamed.

It says POET detective.

I make up rhymes while I solve crimes!

"I don't care how, but I want my diary now!" Emma yelled. "Hey, maybe I'm a poet too."

Marty opened his top secret detective backpack. He took out his green pad and a pen.

"Give me the facts. So I can follow the tracks," he said.

"Well," Emma explained, "my diary is blue. It has a brass lock and key."

Emma showed him the key. It was on a chain around her neck.

I miss my diary already. It's full of all my thoughts and secrets.

Marty wanted to eat his orange. He wanted to sit in the tree and read his poetry book. But business came first.

I'll be glad to look for your missing book.

SEARCHING FOR CLUES

First Marty searched Emma's desk.
He found her markers, her brownie,
her friendship bracelet, her juice
box, her golf ball, her chewed-up
pencil, her eyedropper, even
her collection of Barbie shoes.
But not her diary.

Marty asked Emma when she had seen it last.

"I had it with me at lunch," she said. "I remember because I almost spilled milk on it. I also had it with me when Mr. Ditz told us about the movie. But it wasn't there when the movie was over."

Marty liked the movie they had seen in class. It was about the sun and the moon. When the movie first started, the projector was too low. The solar system shone on the floor.

When Mr. Ditz went to fix the projector, he walked on the moon. After he fixed the projector, the moon filled the screen.

Watching a movie was good. Listening to Mr. Ditz was not. Did someone steal Emma's diary while the classroom was dark? Did someone want to know Emma's secrets?

It was time to ask some questions.

Pete sat in front of Emma in class. He liked to take things. He took Marty's poetry book last week.

"Did you happen to see a small book with lock and key?"

Pete shook his head. "I was too busy tossing paper clips at the screen."

Marty looked around Pete's desk. He found a pile of paper clips.

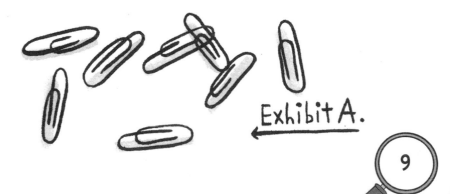

Exhibit A.

9

Marty sat next to Marie.
"Excuse me," Marty said politely.
"I'm busy," Marie answered.
Marty took her crayons away.
"I'll keep it brief. Are you the thief?"
Marie grabbed her crayons back.

Then Marty asked Linda and Tommy and
Luke and Val and Kimmy and Joey the Sneeze
if they saw the diary.

Marty made a list of all the people who might have stolen Emma's diary. Billy Gately was first on the list. He always teased Emma.

Last week he hid a dead butterfly in her tuna fish sandwich.

Emma found it just in time. She thought it was yellow lettuce.

Billy just might be the thief, Marty thought.

"Hello, Mr. Gately. Read any good books lately?" Marty asked.

"No," Billy said. "They ran out of horror books at the library."

Marty leaned in closer.

I was thinking more of a personal story, not the kind that's really gory.

Billy shook his head. "I don't like that kind of stuff."

Marty pulled a blue book from Billy's desk. It was full of scribbled green ink.

Goblins and vampires filled the page.
Billy grabbed the book back.

"Hey, that's my journal for Ms. Barrett's class. What's your problem, anyway?"

Emma whispered to Marty, "My diary is smaller than that. It's a darker shade of blue.

Plus, my handwriting is much neater and I don't draw monsters."

He hated making false arrests.

THE SEARCH CONTINUES

Marty asked Emma if anyone had been looking at her diary.

"Well, Leigh kept asking me about it," Emma said. "She wanted one for her birthday, but she didn't get it."

Leigh was still outside for recess. Marty followed her from the swing set to the hopscotch to the basketball court to the fence to the lunch area.

She pulled a blue book from her bag.
She crouched over on the table and began
to write in the book.

"Aha!" Marty said. "Caught in the act,
and that's a fact! Hand over the diary."

"NO!" Leigh hollered.

She held on to the book with all
her might. So did Marty.

MY Diary

You're in a real dilemma, because this book belongs to Emma.

"Emma?" Leigh asked. "This is *my* diary. I made it from a pad and covered it with blue paper."

She looked at the ground. "I wanted a real diary for my birthday, but I got a bike instead."

Marty didn't feel bad for Leigh. His own bike had a flat tire. He hadn't used it in weeks. He was a good detective but a bad repairman.

Marty apologized to Leigh. He sang her "Happy Birthday" to make up for his mistake.

Emma approached Marty.

"Where's my diary?" she asked. "The whole class could have read it by now."

"I've hit some dead ends, but I hope we're still friends," Marty said.

"We're not!" Emma said.
"I want my money back."

"You gave me no fee. I'm doing this for free," Marty said.

"Well, you're a lousy detective," Emma scolded.

Marty thought and thought. Where was the best place to look for a book? The library, of course. They hurried down the hall. Marty asked the librarian for help.

"Have you seen something small and blue? It's a diary, Mrs. Drew."

I haven't. But have you checked the lost and found?

Marty emptied the box onto a shelf.
He found a left boot, a red mitten, a
broken comb, a nickel (which he claimed),
a bag of acorns, a compass, and a belt.

The closest thing to
a diary was a comic
book. He kept that
for evidence. Mrs. Drew
told Marty the new poetry
books would be in on Friday.

Marty hoped he would solve his case
by then.

"Any luck?" Emma asked.

Marty shook his head. "We don't have
much time. Back to the scene of the crime!"

Marty examined the room again. He took a roll of yellow ribbon from his detective kit. He roped off the area around Emma's desk. Now he could study the crime scene. Maybe he could even dust for fingerprints. Mr. Ditz came back into the classroom. Marty had wanted to solve the case at recess. Now he would have to put in for overtime.

Marty watched everyone take a seat.

He watched Kimmy sit in the back row. She couldn't see the board, so she took a book from the shelf and sat on it like a booster seat.

Maybe the thief wanted Emma's diary for another reason besides reading. Marty suddenly remembered the movie and Mr. Ditz walking on the moon. He hurried to the projector. It was on an empty desk in the middle of the room. It was propped up on a small blue book. Marty lifted the projector. Underneath it was Emma's diary.

Here's your book. There is no crook!

Emma leaped with joy. "My top secret diary. Thank you!"

Mr. Ditz stepped over the yellow ribbon. He looked at the diary.

"Emma, is that yours? I needed a wedge for the projector. Your book was the perfect size. I'm sorry. I should have asked."

Marty handed the book back to Emma.
But it fell on the floor.

SMACK!

When Marty picked
up the diary, the lock was
open. He flipped through
the pages.

"To be perfectly frank, these pages are
blank," Marty said.

"This is embarrassing," Emma confessed.
"I don't really write in my diary. I just like
using the little key."

She put the key in
the lock and turned it.
When it clicked shut,
she smiled.

A JOB WELL DONE

Another case solved. Marty took the orange from his pocket.

Maybe now he could finish his snack and read his poetry book.

"Hey!" Emma pointed to the orange. "I bet you can't think of a rhyme for that!"

Marty peeled the fruit and took a slice.

> Orange is alone in the no-rhyme zone.

He took another bite. Solving cases always made him hungry.

29

THE CASE OF ACTION CHUCK

THE CRIME

Marty walked home from school. He was glad he could help his friend Emma today.

He walked by the hardware store, the clothing store, and the fire station.

He climbed up the tree in front of the ice-cream shop.

It was his favorite view of town.

From his perch, he could see Mr. Lipsky's toy store. Mr. Lipsky stood on the sidewalk. He was shaking his head, looking sad. Marty climbed down the tree and walked over. He asked Mr. Lipsky what was wrong.

I'm missing a box of toys.

They were brand-new Action Chuck dolls.

Marty couldn't believe it! Marty loved Action Chuck! Action Chuck was a truck driver on TV. He drove around the country and stopped bad guys. Marty watched his show every week.

Marty gave Mr. Lipsky a smile and said, "Mr. Lipsky, with some luck, you'll soon be holding Action Chuck."

Marty followed Mr. Lipsky inside. The store was full of giant panda dolls, woodpecker puzzles, baseball bats, skateboards, polka-dot beach balls, magic tricks, and poster paints. But most of all, the store was full of people. Some waited in line, some waited for help. Some waited to play with toys.

LIZARD BOY

Magic TRicKS→

Can I
get him?
Can I?
Can I?

"If you give me the scoop, I can start to snoop," Marty told Mr. Lipsky.

"The truck came after lunch," Mr. Lipsky explained. "They delivered six boxes. Two boxes were filled with puppets, another with books. The fourth box was full of games and balloons, and the last two were Action Chuck boxes." Mr. Lipsky walked over to a stack of boxes.

"Now there's only one box of Action Chucks."

Mr. Lipsky opened a box with his knife and took out an Action Chuck doll. Marty's favorite—the one with the driving gloves and removable sunglasses.

"Twenty-four of these dolls are missing," Mr. Lipsky said. "I can't get another shipment for two months. So many children will be disappointed."

Marty asked Mr. Lipsky who else was working in the store.

"My son, Peter, and a new boy, Tom," he answered.

Marty got up from his chair.

Let's get to work. Where's the new clerk?

r. Lipsky and Marty found Tom. He was stacking shelves with games. Mr. Lipsky introduced Tom to Marty, then turned to help a customer. Marty waved and Tom climbed down the ladder.

"Where were you today around two?" Marty asked.

"I was here," Tom answered. "Helping Mr. Lipsky with the new shipment."

"When you unloaded the truck, did you see Action Chuck?" Marty asked.

Tom got very excited. "Action Chuck is the greatest!" he said. "My friends and I watch his show all the time."

Marty and Tom talked about how cool Action Chuck was. They talked about the two-way radio in his thermos. They talked about the secret laser in his rearview mirror. Then Marty remembered he was supposed to be solving a case.

"I must find the crate before it's too late," he declared.

Marty looked around. He liked this store. He liked Mr. Lipsky's other store too. It was near Marty's grandmother's house. Sometimes she took Marty there for a treat.

Marty always pretended he didn't want anything. His grandmother always bought him something anyway.

Mr. Lipsky finished with his customer. "Let's go find my son."

He took Marty into the back room.

"Peter!" he called.

No one answered.

"That's strange," Mr. Lipsky said. "He should be here."

"I'll sit and wait. He won't be late," Marty said.

"Good idea," Mr. Lipsky replied.

"Describe your son so I'll know he's the one," Marty rhymed. Mr. Lipsky told Marty his son had brown glasses, blond hair, and a beard.

Then Mr. Lipsky went back into the store. Marty waited for Peter Lipsky.

While he waited, Marty looked around. He looked on the shelves. He looked in the closet. There were lots of action figures but no **Action Chucks.** He checked the bulletin board. There were notes reminding Mr. Lipsky to order new games. Notes reminding him to bring toys to the other store. Notes reminding him to call his son. Mr. Lipsky needs a lot of reminding, Marty thought. Marty sat on a box

41

and took out his poetry book, the new one
with poems about railroads.

A few minutes later, Tom came into
the room.

Marty hid behind a box. He took his
spyglass from his backpack. He'd made it
with old tubes and foil. He watched Tom
dial the phone.

"The action figures are ready," Tom said.
"You can pick them up tonight."

Tom hung up the phone. Marty popped
up from behind the box.

"You should have confessed. Now you're under arrest!"

What are you talking about? That was the children's hospital. We have boxes of old toys to give them.

Marty felt bad he had blamed Tom. But he was glad the hospital would get some toys.

Marty returned to snooping. Soon he heard a noise outside. He pulled a box over to the window to stand on. Marty searched the parking lot. He saw a young man with blond hair and a beard. He wore glasses. This must be Peter Lipsky. He was putting a large box into the trunk of his car. Marty tiptoed outside to get a better look.

Marty hid behind the stairs. He watched Mr. Lipsky's son tie down the box. The stamp on the side of the box said:

Marty ran across the parking lot. He looked Peter in the eye and said, "You can't steal from your dad. That would be bad."

Marty yelled to Mr. Lipsky in the store. Mr. Lipsky hurried outside. Peter tried to explain but Marty interrupted and told him to be quiet. He opened the trunk of the car. He showed the box to Mr. Lipsky. Mr. Lipsky was very mad.

"Where are you taking these?" he asked his son.

Peter sat Mr. Lipsky down on the stairs.

"You left me a note," Peter said. "You told me to take this box to the other store."

Mr. Lipsky scratched his head. "I don't remember that," he said.

Peter took a note out of his pocket. He showed it to his father. He showed it to Marty. It said:

Mr. Lipsky studied the note.

"I guess I did write that," he said. "I'm so busy, I forgot."

Peter gave his father a smile. "It's okay," he said.

Peter looked at Marty. Peter was not smiling.

"I would not steal from my father," Peter said.

Marty wished he had not wrongly accused Peter. But he was glad he found the missing toys.

He held out his hand. Peter shook it. This time, Peter and Marty both smiled.

A JOB WELL DONE

Marty helped Peter pack up the box in the car.

"Wait a minute," Mr. Lipsky said. He took out his knife. He opened the box. He took out an Action Chuck doll and handed it to Marty. "Thanks for helping me find these," he said.

Marty beamed. On his way out, Marty had an idea. "Maybe I can do something more. I'd like to help you in your store."

Mr. Lipsky told Marty he could stop by anytime. "We need all the help we can get."

Marty told Mr. Lipsky he would see him tomorrow. Then he walked toward home. He was glad Action Chuck was with him. Not that he needed any help stopping crime.

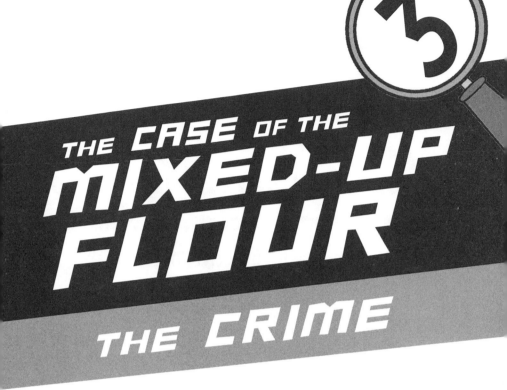

THE CASE OF THE MIXED-UP FLOUR

THE CRIME

Marty read his poetry book and ate his after-school snack. (Chocolate cookies and milk.) Action Chuck sat on the table. Marty's mother mixed butter and sugar in a bowl. She turned on the oven. She asked Marty about his day. He told her about

finding Emma's diary. He told her about
helping Mr. Lipsky at the toy store.

"Sounds like a busy day," his mother said.

Marty's sister, Katie, ran into the room.
Her hair was red. Every other day, her hair
was blond. Marty figured she had been
painting. He was a detective, after all.

Someone took
my flour!

It was a
present from
Jackie!

"I haven't seen it," Mrs. Frye said.
"Maybe it's in your room."

"No," Katie said. "It was on the table.
Now it's gone!"

Marty looked
at the clock.

I might have time
for one more crime.

He took his plate to the sink. He washed
his hands. He followed Katie downstairs to
the playroom.

SEARCHING FOR CLUES

Marty took out his pad. He told Katie to tell him everything. Katie took a deep breath.

"Jackie and I painted after school," she explained.

Katie showed Marty their paintings. One looked like a clown with dandruff. Another looked like a car with mice.

"Then we decided to make some goop," Katie continued. "Jackie brought over a bag of flour."

Marty had seen Katie make goop before. She squished it between her fingers. She put

food coloring in it. She made a giant mess. It was not his idea of fun. But he still had to help his sister. He looked around the room.

"This place is clean for a goopy crime scene," he said.

"Before we even started, someone took the flour," Katie said.

Marty checked the door. It was unlocked.

We better work fast. When did you see it last?

"About five," Katie answered. "When Jackie's mother called her home."

The last time Marty saw Jackie, she was juggling garlic and roller-skating at the same time.

"I think she's wacky, but let's talk to Jackie," Marty said.

Marty and Katie walked next door.

Jackie's mother answered the door.

"Jackie's in her room," she said.
Marty and Katie went inside.

Jackie was playing her trombone.
She wore purple rain boots and a striped
ski hat.

"I'm practicing for band," Jackie
explained.

You can play all day,
but we can't stay.

"Why do you rhyme all the time? It gets on my nerves," Jackie said.

Marty didn't mention how he felt about her hat. He asked Jackie if she had seen Katie's flour.

"Yes," Jackie answered. "I gave it to her. We were going to make goop."

"Pardon the poem, but did you take it home?" Marty asked.

"Of course not," Jackie said. "The flour was a present."

Marty whispered to Katie, "She may be unique, but I don't think she's a sneak."

He decided to leave before Jackie played another song.

Marty and Katie walked past Mr. Lynch's house. Marty saw something on the ground. It was a trail of white powder. He bent down and touched it.

"It might be flour, but it smells a bit sour," Marty said.

He and Katie followed the trail. It led to Mr. Lynch's backyard. Mr. Lynch was planting tulips. Next to him was a bag that looked like flour. Marty knelt down beside him. He pointed to the bag. He pointed to Katie.

Excuse me, sir. Did you take this from her?

Mr. Lynch shook his head. "This is a special mix," he answered. "It helps the flowers grow."

He sprinkled some powder in the soil.

Marty remembered a poem he had read that morning. It was about tulips growing along the railroad tracks.

He wanted to stay and watch Mr. Lynch, but Katie started to walk home.

Mr. Lynch had something, yes indeed. A mixture to help his flowers seed.

You're the **WORST** brother, the **WORST** poet, and the **WORST** detective in the world!

It was always difficult keeping a little sister happy.

Marty told Katie they should keep looking, but first he wanted to track down a clue. He remembered his mother was baking. He remembered that flour went into cake. Maybe his mom took Katie's by mistake. (Sometimes he even thought in rhymes.)

Mom, we've been looking for an hour. Have you seen Katie's flour?

His mother opened the oven door. She took out a beautiful yellow cake.

"I haven't seen it," his mother said. "What was it in?"

His mother must have a lot on her mind. Even more than Mr. Lipsky. Marty told her the flour was in a bag.

"When you find it, make sure you put it in some water," she said.

Marty sighed. Even his mother wanted to make goop. As he left the kitchen, he wondered if he should take the cake as evidence.

He decided to wait until he solved the case. He ran outside to find Katie. Marty told Katie he was still looking.

"Forget it," Katie said. "You're fired!"

Katie ran into
the house.

Marty ran to his favorite tree.
He climbed to his favorite branch.
(Climbing and rhyming were the
best things in the world.) Right now
he needed to think. He wanted to
help his sister, but his leads were
running out.

Finally Marty had a plan. He would search the house from the attic to the basement. He would open every drawer, every cupboard. He would solve this case. From the tree, he could see Mr. Lynch's yard. Mr. Lynch was still planting flowers. They lined the fence in yellow and red. FLOWERS! Marty had an idea.

He ran into the house. He brought Katie into the kitchen. He asked his mother again if she had seen Katie's flour.

"No, I haven't," his mother answered. "But we can pick another one tomorrow."

Marty opened the cupboard.

He pointed to a bag of flour.

Marty sang, "Here's how I solved this tricky case—Mom thought your flour went in a vase!"

His mother looked at the bag.

"Katie, I thought you lost a *flower*. I thought you were looking for a rose or a daisy."

Now Marty understood why his mother told him to put the flour in water.

"I needed the flour to make a cake," his mother said. "I didn't know it was yours, Katie."

"Thanks, Marty," Katie said. "Maybe you're not the worst brother after all."

Katie took the bag to the playroom. She poured the flour into a bowl of water. She made a gooey mess. Katie was happy. Marty was too. He cut himself a huge piece of cake and opened his poetry book.

It was his just dessert.

A JOB WELL DONE

After dinner and homework, Marty went to bed. Action Chuck shared his pillow, just in case any bad guys showed up in his dreams. Marty's mother came into the room.

> You solved three cases today. Soon you won't have time for school.

Really?

Marty jumped up in bed.

"No, not really," his mother answered.
She tucked Marty back in.

"Maybe tomorrow there will be another case," Marty said.

"Maybe some brand-new clues to chase," his mother added.

"Hey," Marty said. "You're a poet too!"

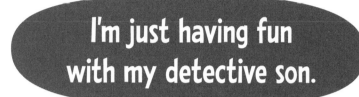

I'm just having fun with my detective son.

Then she kissed Marty and shut off the light.

Marty went to sleep. He dreamed that
Action Chuck poured goop along the railroad
tracks. He dreamed the bad guys read
poems until the police came. He smiled in
his sleep.

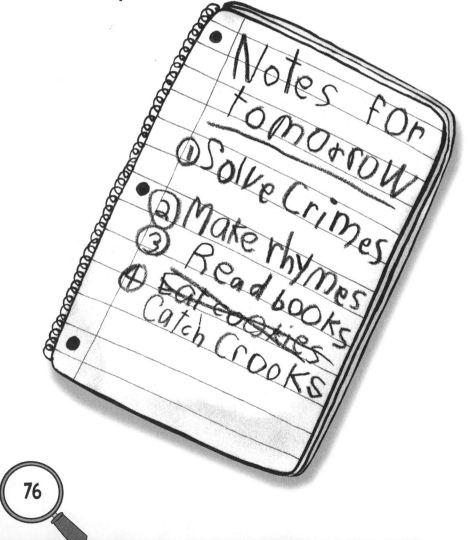

TURN THE PAGE FOR A SNEAK PEEK AT THE NEXT

MARTY FRYE PRIVATE EYE

ADVENTURE

BOOK TWO

THE **CASE** OF THE **STOLEN POODLE** & OTHER MYSTERIES

THE CASE OF THE STOLEN CANDY

THE CRIME

On the walk home from school, Marty took off his backpack and climbed his favorite tree. The giant maple had lots of thick branches. From his perch, Marty had a great view of the park, town hall, fire station, pizza parlor, candy store, and pet shop. Lots of people were gathered at the fire station, probably for a field trip.

Aren't you that poet detective?

Marty looked down from his perch to see Mr. Hammond from the candy store.

"My famous hot jawbreakers have been stolen! Hundreds of dollars' worth—GONE!" Mr. Hammond said.

Marty scrambled out of the tree. His afternoon break would have to wait.

Marty followed Mr. Hammond to the candy store. It was one of his favorite places, with rows and rows of colorful penny candy. Lollipops, gum, candy necklaces, licorice, and fudge. The store carried everything a kid with a sweet tooth could want.

Marty took out his notebook. "I'm here to snoop—so give me the scoop."

Mr. Hammond nervously wrung his apron as he spoke. "Felix Dupont, the food critic from the local paper, is coming to write an article about the store—

especially our super hot jawbreakers.
What am I going to do? I ran to the bank
and when I came back, all the jawbreakers
were gone."

Marty popped a lemon sourball into his mouth. If he was going to solve this crime, he'd need to study the evidence.

Marty checked the locks on both doors but neither was broken. He asked Mr. Hammond if a customer might be involved instead of a burglar.

"The only customer I have trouble with is Jerome. He tries to sneak candy into his pockets all the time." Mr. Hammond looked around the store. "But I never thought he'd take every last jawbreaker."

Marty wrote this fact into his notebook. He also continued to look around the store. Something was definitely wrong.

Marty pointed to the tile floor. It was perfectly neat, with no sign of discarded wrappers.

This place is clean for a robbery scene.

Mr. Hammond didn't
have time to answer Marty
because a tall man with a
beard and a tape recorder
entered the store. Mr.
Hammond pulled Marty
aside. "It's Felix Dupont
the food critic—and I
don't have any
jawbreakers!"

The critic introduced
himself to Mr. Hammond and Marty. He
asked if the photographer had arrived
yet. Mr. Hammond said no and led the
critic to the fudge.

From his place behind the chocolate coins, Marty spied on Mr. Dupont.

The food critic was also writing in a spiral notebook. Marty wasn't sure he trusted this guy. Did Mr. Dupont know more about Mr. Hammond's store than he was letting on?